To the real Delphi, with much love, special girl ~ L G

For John, Laurie and James ~ P M

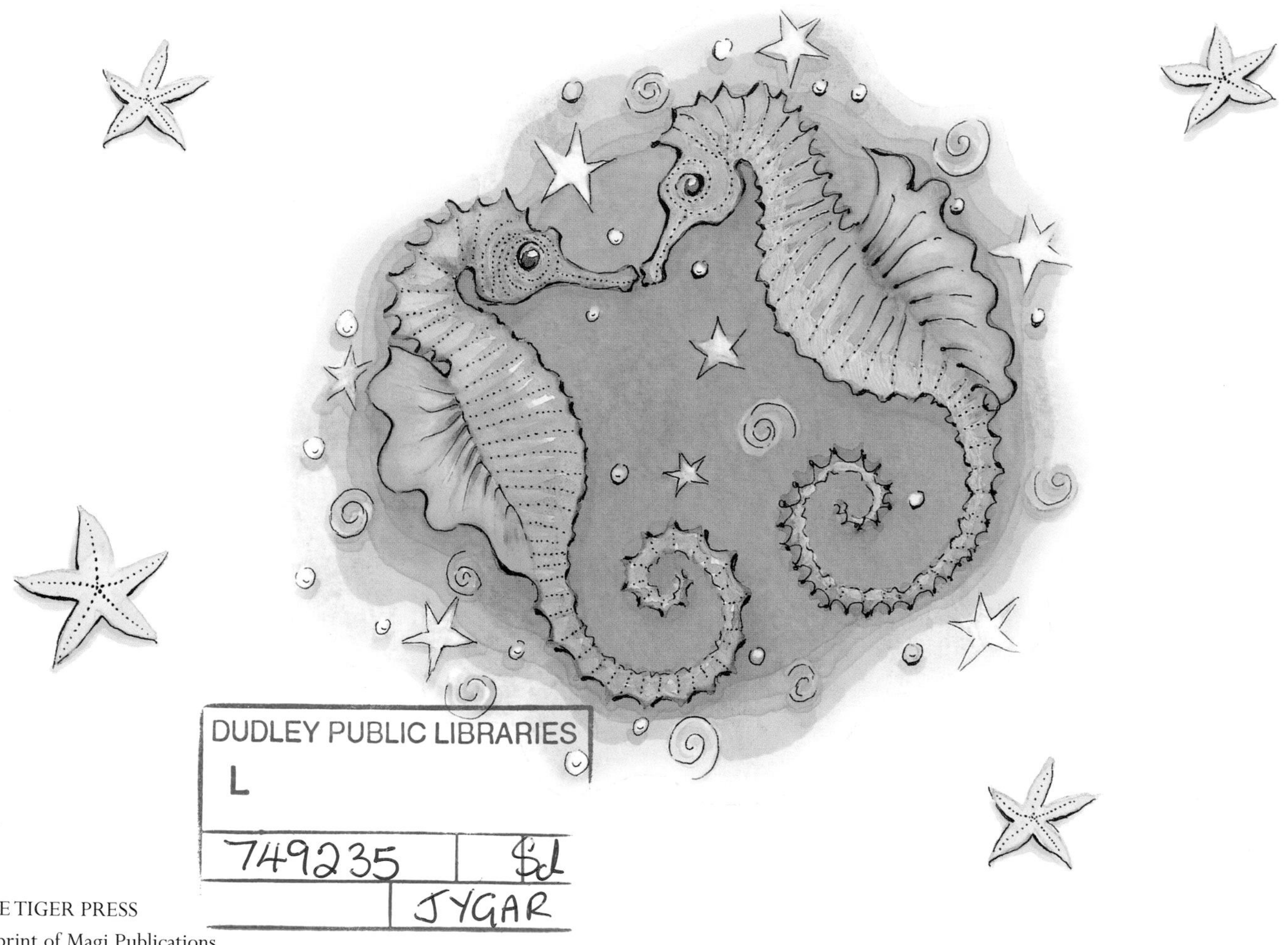

LITTLE TIGER PRESS
An imprint of Magi Publications
1 The Coda Centre, 189 Munster Road, London SW6 6AW
www.littletigerpress.com

First published in Great Britain 2006

A CIP catalogue record for this book is available from the British Library

 • ISBN 1 84506 259 0

Printed in Singapore by Tien Wah Press Pte.

10 9 8 7 6 5 4 3 2 1

The Tiniest Mermaid

Laura Garnham

Illustrated by

Patricia MacCarthy

LITTLE TIGER PRESS
London

"I wish I were a mermaid," said Lily one night.

"It is wonderful," Delphi said wistfully. "My friends and I travel the whole world using our magic to help trapped or hurt animals. And sometimes we use our sparkling tails to guide sailors home through terrible storms."

"Wow!" said Lily in wonder. "I never knew!"

"It's exciting, but it can be very scary," said Delphi. "When I was hurt in that awful storm, I was separated from my friends by a huge wave and thrown on to the rocks." She sighed. "They must be wondering what happened to me."

Lily gasped. Delphi's friends would be so worried about her!

"Oh Delphi," she cried. "You must go back to your friends!"

"Yes, I must," said Delphi. "But I shall miss you."

"If only we didn't have to say goodbye!" sighed Lily. "I wish I could come with you. Or just visit your magical world."

Delphi smiled suddenly. "I could show you, if you like. Close your eyes . . ."

Lily took a deep breath as Delphi started singing a gentle, lilting song. Lily could feel magic all round her and hear the rush of the ocean growing louder . . .

All at once she was there with Delphi, swimming with dolphins as they danced and dived through the water.

Further and further they swam through the warm blue ocean until the setting sun turned the white beaches gold.

When Lily fell asleep that night she could still hear the whale's song and feel the sand between her toes.

The next morning Lily cradled Delphi in her hands for the very last time as she carried her to the seashore.

“Don’t be sad, Lily,” said Delphi softly, and she gave her a special shell. “Whenever you miss me,” she said, “put the shell to your ear and you will hear the magic of the sea whispering inside.”

With a flick of her glittering tail, the tiny mermaid swam off. But as she waved goodbye Lily saw two more shining tails appear at Delphi's side. Delphi was with her friends and she was safe. And Lily knew that whenever she missed her she could listen to the sounds of the shell and look for the sparkles glimmering in the sea, for Delphi would always be near.